THE

I NEVER

ASHLEY-RAE STEWART

Fulton Books, Inc.
Meadville, PA

Published by Fulton Books 2017

ISBN 978-1-63338-296-1 (Paperback)
ISBN 978-1-63338-575-7 (Hard Cover)
ISBN 978-1-63338-297-8 (Digital)

Printed in the United States of America

Chapter 1

WHY!

"C'mon, Kelly, the moving truck will be here soon," said Kelly's mother.

"But I love it here in Montana. We've lived here for five whole years! I'm going to miss it. I'm going to miss the farm animals dearly, especially Bailey. She is a great horse, and now we'll have to sell her to some stranger. I will have to go back to being in a city but not in New York, which I knew very well. Oh how I miss when Dad used to take me to the best ice cream parlor in the world every Sunday. Now everything will be different. Mama, why does Papa hate me?" Kelly asked.

"What do you mean? Papa found a great job in California. You will be able to make new friends and participate in new activities at your new school. You are very unique. So *relax*!" said Mrs. Netti.

"But what about bullies? I need a makeover. I need cool clothes!" said Kelly.

"What you need is Papa's special recipe for homemade hot chocolate! It's too bad we can't make it now because all of our utensils are probably on a plane to the new house. All you need to do is just take a deep breath and be strong," suggested Mrs. Netti. "Most of the time, people are so worried about the future that they don't get to enjoy the beautiful things that are going on right now. Sweetheart, all you need to do is believe in yourself. You need to believe that you are Kelly Gordon-Netti, and there is no one else like you. You are one of a kind so give me a kiss and forget about the drama."

Kelly sighed, then said, "Fine."

Kelly lied down and stared into the blue sky. She thought of all the great times she had in Montana. She remembered being at the park and her dad pushing her high on the swings.

And how her dad would sing to her when she felt sad. She thought about Rikki's Pizza Palace, which she believed had the best pizza in America, but her all-time favorite place was Splash World Water Park. It had awesome rides, a lazy river, and cotton candy in every color.

She stood up to say good-bye to the animals before a farmer came to pick them up. She looked at the chickens and said her goodbyes to Henry, Mason, Chuckles, and Walter, the newest additions to the farm family. She bid the hens and the cows farewell and walked over to the stables to say goodbye to her dear horses Dana, Blue, Dove, Sky, and her favorite Bailey. Bailey was a white horse with white hair. Kelly loved her because she knew her the longest — five years to be exact, and because she was the most daring horse to ride. It pained Kelly to see her go.

Kelly returned to the house to greet her two best friends — Lola and Kristina. They hugged, they cried, and they talked on the front porch until it was time for Kelly to leave. "Remember the time we conquered our fear of heights, or when we had our first slumber party?" Lola cracked a joke to uplift everyone's mood as she always did. Kelly gave them both handcrafted bracelets to remember her by.

Later on, when Kelly reached the airport, her dad was already there to get all the luggage sorted out. Kelly's dad asked her, "Are you mad at me?"

Kelly answered, "Not as much anymore."

Her dad gave her a big kiss on the cheek.

Before heading to the gate, Kelly and her parents went to a food court to have lunch. They asked Kelly what she wanted, but she didn't answer. So her mom ordered spaghetti and meatballs because that was one of Kelly's favorite meals. She also bought a colorful lollipop with swirls to cheer her up.

When the food came, Kelly pushed it away. She put her head down and just sat there like a bag of potatoes. It was clear that Kelly would miss her home. Her life was about to change and she didn't feel quite ready.

Suddenly, Kelly's dad stood up. She knew he was going to sing the Kelly song. This song always made her laugh growing up. As he got up, Kelly mumbled, "Dad, sit down. You're embarrassing me."

He sang.

OHHHHH

When I come down the road what do I see.

Kelly Gordon-Netti staring at me.

I smile at her, she smiles back.

Life is so wonderful. Why don't you pack?

Let's go on an adventure.

We have such a good day.

This deserves a hooray.

And I don't have much more to say.

"Feel better, honey bun?" Kelly's dad asked.

"Sure do feel a little embarrassed, but that song will always rule," Kelly replied.

Kelly's parents wrapped up the food and put it in a bag, which they would save for Kelly until they got on the plane. When Kelly boarded the plane, she pulled out a pocket journal. She started writing about how she felt, because it seemed like no one fully understood her pain. She would miss out on everything. Little did she know that within a few days those feelings would go away.

In her journal, she wrote,

> *No one understands what I'm going through. I want to stay. Maybe I could stay with Kristina or Lola for a few days. I would be an excellent house guest. I'll miss all my childhood memories. Does Mom and Dad think that a kiss on the cheek is going to drive the tears away? They are so rude for acting like this is not a big deal. They are taking so much away from me.*

> *I am even going to miss that weird girl across the street. Uggh this is the worst!*

> *Man! I wonder how Bailey is doing.*

> *I miss her.*

The plane took off, and Kelly looked sadly through the window and whispered, "Bye, Montana."

Kelly went to sleep and eventually started to dream. She dreamt of what she thought would happen when she arrived in Los Angeles. Kelly dreamt of having a nice house and lots of sunny days. She also dreamt of friendly people and new adventures.

She woke up to the flight attendant's voice who was offering her a bag of salted crunchy nuts and apple juice. "No, thank you," she said.

She asked her mom to give her the food that she had refused to eat earlier. "Feeling better, honey?" Her mom asked. Kelly looked at her and smiled.

Kelly took the fork and spun it round in a circle and slurped her spaghetti until it was finished. Then she plugged in her headphones into her iPod and listened to some music.

When she had eaten the spaghetti and meatballs, she looked out the window and couldn't believe how beautiful everything looked. She picked up her journal again. She wrote,

We are almost there! I can see the beach and the palm trees. Why was I worried again?

It's so beautiful. I hope they have a mall and amusement parks with roller coasters, water rides, and a Ferris wheel. I also see a lot of buildings. Wow, I think I'm going to like this place.

Her California adventure had officially begun.

Chapter 2

THE NEW KID

Kelly Gordon-Netti was now the new kid in town. She was a nice young lady with brown hair and brown eyes. She wore glasses and always had her hair in cute curly round pigtails. Her family was half-Jamaican and half-South Korean. Though only 11 years old, she was a talented steel drum and soccer player, and singer. As an only child, she got a lot of attention at home which was part of the reason she had done so well in school.

Kelly had been accepted to the Woodrow Intermediate School in Los Angeles, California.

On the first day of school. Kelly woke up at 6:00 a.m. to the sound of her alarm clock. She took a shower, brushed her teeth with blue mint-scented toothpaste, and put on a blue plaid shirt and khaki pants. She then went to the kitchen where her mom made her waffles with scrambled eggs and turkey bacon.

"Ready for school, my dear?" Kelly's mom asked as she packed her lunchbox with a turkey sandwich, water, a juice box, and a bag of cheese curls. The school bus honked outside as Kelly's mom kissed her good-bye.

When Kelly arrived at school, she felt excited. She met Mrs. K the music teacher, Mr. Morris the math teacher, Ms. Allen the history teacher, and Ms. Singh the English teacher who all seemed really nice.

She had been assigned to locker 133. Kelly pulled out some supplies to decorate her locker because the bus had dropped her off a bit early. She posted stickers and pictures of her family and friends, and hung a calendar to remember important dates. "Perfect," she said when the task was completed.

Kelly looked around her and attempted to say hello to her classmates. However, it appeared that friend groups had already been formed. Some students waved at each other while others cracked a smile; but no one stopped to acknowledge her.

Kelly refused to let this bother her. Kelly had always dreamed of becoming a doctor, so she would work hard to achieve that.

Kelly longed for best friends like Lola and Kristina. She was alone most of the time while at school. She sat by herself at lunch, walked down the hallways by herself, and spent recess alone. When she would try to talk to some of the other kids, they didn't respond because they said she was different from everyone else. But Kelly didn't see it that way, because being different is what made her special.

When she came home after school one day, she went to her room and cried. Her dad knocked on her door and asked, "What's wrong, pumpkin?"

"I don't have any friends," she cried.

Her dad said, "I am your friend."

She said, "I know, but I want someone like me that I can talk to."

Her dad sighed, "All right, I do believe that very soon you will have good friends who will love and respect you. In the meantime, I will get you something to cheer you up," and then he left the room. He thought it would be a good idea to get her a golden retriever because it was her favorite canine breed. He discussed the idea with mom before going to sleep that night, and she agreed.

One hot morning as the birds were singing, and the sun was shining brightly, Kelly began to panic because she was running late for school. The battery in the alarm clock had stopped working so it never rang. She woke up thirty minutes late and rushed to catch the bus. She didn't have time to eat her breakfast, so she brought it on the bus with her. She was eating quietly when Tony Cruzer, one of the meanest boys in school, walked up to her and yelled, "Give me that seat, *nerd*!"

"No!" said Kelly.

Tony grabbed Kelly's breakfast and threw it across the bus. Kelly stood up and moved to the back seat because she remembered her parents telling her that if she did good things, good things would happen.

When Kelly arrived at school she was very hungry and started to feel sick. Because of that, she was distracted and didn't answer many of the questions asked in class as she usually did.

"Kelly!" Ms. Thomas said abruptly, "where is Latin America?"

Kelly moaned in discomfort.

"Are you okay Kelly?" Ms. Thomas asked in concern.

Kelly shook her head indicating no, so Ms. Thomas sent Kelly to the nurse. She told the nurse what had happened and the school called Tony's parents. He was given one week of detention as punishment. Kelly was then allowed to go to lunch early.

Later that afternoon a sign-up sheet was posted for the reading club. It grabbed Kelly's attention, so she signed her name. The head of the cheerleading squad, Amelia Radison, happened to pass by and scoffed at her; but Kelly didn't care. 'What goes around comes around,' she thought. Kelly noticed that she was the third person on the list. The first two people on the list were two kids with good grades.

Book Club

Dear students, if you would like to join the book club this year, please sign your names below:

1. Alison Sajin
2. Mikel Webster
3. Kelly Gordon-Netti

We will meet at 3:00 p.m. after school, Monday–Friday.

Thank you,
School Activities Committee

The next day, there was an assembly at Kelly's school. Principal Robert stood up and spoke about elections for Student Council. He spoke about the positions like president, vice president and so on, and about the expectations for serving on the council.

Kelly thought about signing up so that she could prove to the bullies that she was a valuable member of the student body with big aspirations. As she marched to the sign-up sheet she heard Amelia Redison snicker, "You don't have a chance!"

Kelly answered, "We'll just have to wait and see what happens."

Amelia answered, "You are the new kid, you better watch yourself, or you're going to get hurt. I can get all the support I need."

Kelly turned around, her pigtails whipping across Amelia's face, to read the names on the paper. Unfazed by the competition, she rushed home to share the news with her parents.

Student Council Sign-up Sheet

1. Tony Cruzer Vice PRESIDENT

2. *Alise Panner   Secretary*

3. Amelia Redison   President

4. Taylor Edison   Clerk

5. Kelly Gordon- Netti   President

6. Kenny Mason Treasurer

7. Victoria Watson Clerk

8. Victor Watson Treasurer

9. Charles Antor   ~~Secratery~~
Secretary

10. Tyler Timber   Vice President

She came rushing home with a big smile on her face. "What happened?" Her dad asked, and she told him about the sign-up sheet. He said, "I have an even bigger surprise for you." Then her mom appeared holding a golden retriever puppy. Kelly was so excited, she squealed.

She felt like the happiest girl in the world in that moment. She said, " I will name him Maxwell–Max for short."

Her parents told her that Max was almost two weeks old and would be growing very quickly. They gave her instructions on how to care for him on a small piece of paper.

The paper read,

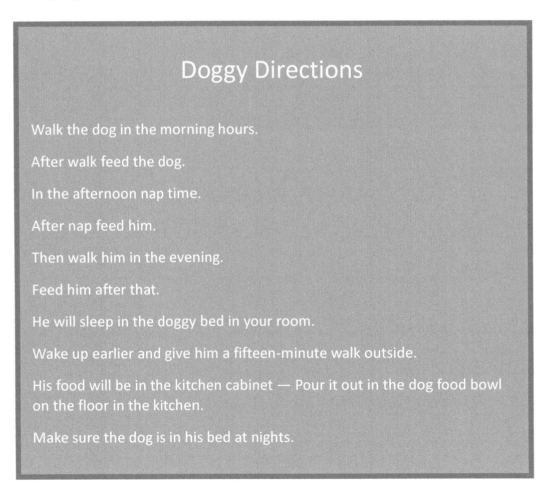

Doggy Directions

Walk the dog in the morning hours.

After walk feed the dog.

In the afternoon nap time.

After nap feed him.

Then walk him in the evening.

Feed him after that.

He will sleep in the doggy bed in your room.

Wake up earlier and give him a fifteen-minute walk outside.

His food will be in the kitchen cabinet — Pour it out in the dog food bowl on the floor in the kitchen.

Make sure the dog is in his bed at nights.

At dinnertime, Kelly poured out puppy chow into Max's bowl. Then she whistled his name. She was surprised that he responded so quickly. Kelly sat at the table, and they said grace. Kelly started to eat her chicken and veggies. Max left his chow and came to the table to beg. She tossed him a carrot stick. Her mom noticed and said, "Don't give your vegetables to the dog just because you don't want to eat them."

"Your mom is right. Don't you want to get tall and strong?" Her dad said.

Kelly rolled her eyes and drank some punch.

Later on, as Kelly studied in her bean bag chair, her mom brought her a snack, half of a turkey sandwich with cheese curls. Her mom said, "I thought you could use a break." She discussed Kelly's new responsibilities as a dog owner.

Kelly felt fully prepared for the new challenge.

"I got this," she said boldly.

"Sweetie, it is not as easy as you think," her mom remarked.

'How hard can it be?' Kelly wondered.

Chapter 3

THE CAMPAIGN

Kelly worked diligently on making posters for her campaign. Her dad helped her write a speech, and her mom helped her make buttons, and bake cookies and cupcakes. Her classmates noticed and uttered, "I'll vote for you if you give me another cookie," and "I'll wear your badge around if you give me another cupcake."

Kelly obliged but reminded them to vote for the person they thought would make the best president. She wanted to be fair.

Kelly quickly became a baking sensation. She baked goodies for the basketball team and the cheerleaders. She baked for the teachers to support the school's fundraisers. All this attention made Amelia mad.

Kelly was doing very well with her campaign until her opponent, Amelia Radison, started to make mean cheers about Kelly during cheerleading practice. But Kelly was a nice girl. She also made the smart decision to list all the reasons she felt she would make a good president. She posted copies of it all around the school campus.

The following week elections were held in the auditorium. Tony Cruzer was booed off the stage because he was a bully, and so was Amelia Redison for the same reason. When Kelly appeared on stage, Tony gave her a mean look remembering the week of detention he received because of her. Then, he punched his hand to intimidate her. Kelly stood up and everyone clapped because she had launched the best campaign. At the end of her speech she received a rousing round of applause.

A week later, the results were posted. Kelly had won the presidency. When Amelia saw the results, she screamed in horror and threw a tantrum.

"Kelly! Kelly! Kelly!" the school cheered when she entered the cafeteria. This made Amelia feel quite angry, so she conspired with her cheerleading squad to embarrass her. But the first thing Kelly did as president was to collaborate with administrators in an effort to put an end to bullying. There were new penalties for bullying and administrators were now on high alert for hostile behavior.

She also organized class trips to museums and theme parks. She greeted everyone with either a smile or a "what's up?" She soon became not only well-known but also well-liked by everyone, except for Tony and Amelia.

Amelia delivered a passionate speech to her squad about how Kelly was a threat and should be viewed as an enemy, not a friend. Together they wrote a mean cheer and choreography to go along with it.

At the biggest basketball game of the season they formed a circle around Kelly and cheered:

Kelly, Kelly, you're so rude.

Kelly, you look like a dude

You're crazy

You're lazy

Don't be sad

Don't get mad

Smelly Kelly, shoo!!

Kelly left the court in tears. "How could they be so cruel?" she cried.

When the guidance counselor heard what had happened she gave the whole cheerleading squad detention and lectured them on the importance of being kind and respectful. She also told them that engaging in community service would be a new requirement for all teams including their squad. Though they were not thrilled to hear this, they felt worse about embarrassing Kelly at the basketball game. They had neglected their responsibilities as cheerleaders and endeavored to be better about spreading school spirit.

When Kelly got home, a plate of lasagna with a side salad was waiting for her. She recounted the events of the day as tears of anger and sadness ran down her cheeks.

Her mom said, "It's all about what you think your purpose is. You've been doing such a great job as president. Don't let this hinder you from fulfilling your purpose. Those girls can't go through life being bullies. That's why your new initiative is so important."

She dried Kelly's tears.

Kelly took a deep breath. She knew her mom was right, so she gave her a tight hug and gave thanks for her meal.

Chapter 4

THE TALENT SHOW

The school was buzzing about the upcoming talent show. The posters that went up read:-

**Come One, Come All
To The Talent Showcase
November 11th @
4:30 p.m. In The Auditorium**

For more information, contact KELLY GORDON NETTI

When the day finally came, all seventeen performers gathered backstage to rehearse. Parents filled the auditorium. Kelly emerged in a beautiful sparkly dress to deliver the opening remarks. Although she was the emcee, she was also taking part in the show. One trophy would be awarded in each category of music, dance, gymnastics, and unusual talents. Amelia and Kelly found themselves in the same category. Amelia would sing and Kelly would play the bagpipes.

When the show began, the first people to go up were Victoria Watson with her brother Victor. They sang "The Mouse and the Cheese" and Victoria dressed up in a grey mouse costume with whiskers and buck teeth, and Victor wore a cheese costume. Victoria danced around Victor on the stage. Their performance was hilarious. The judges and the audience laughed throughout the whole presentation.

Kelly had to introduce the next contestant so she said, "Next up is the one and only Amelia Redison who we all know and love." Amelia wore an evening dress with high heels that she kept tripping over. She sang a song that she had written about herself called "Me" (as the title implies). As she sang, she moved around the stage. After the first verse, her heels got caught in her dress and she tripped and fell. The feedback from the microphone startled the crowd. She felt humiliated because people were booing and laughing. She took her shoes off and ran off the stage as fast as she could. Kelly felt sorry for her.

But it was now Kelly's turn to play the steel drums. She played this entertaining piece that her dad taught her. The judges enjoyed the selection, and the audience seemed very amused.

Next up was Eddy. He played a really slow song on his piano which unfortunately seemed to make the audience fall asleep.

The time came for deliberations by the judges. Kelly won the shiny gold first place trophy. In close second were the Watsons who won the silver second place trophy.

The next category of the show was dance. Jackie Smith danced to the Cha-Cha Slide. It was fun at first, but then the audience got bored after a while. The next contestant, Sandy Wright, performed a segment of *Swan Lake* 'en pointe'. Abigail, the last contestant, did the wobble. She moved and grooved with charisma, and she entertained the crowd. Abigail won first place in the dance category, with Sandy coming in as a close second.

Next was gymnastics. Amelia changed into her cheerleading outfit. The cheerleading squad went up first for this category. They did a series of cheers which were really exciting and included flips, splits and tricks. They even rhymed. Three other girls performed a routine, but the overall winners were the cheerleaders.

The final category was miscellaneous. The first boy, Jimmy Martinez, performed ventriloquism with his puppet. It was super funny and the crowd laughed as Jimmy and his puppet called each other names. The next person, Ricky, burped the ABCs and the crowd booed. Maya drank two large bottles of water in less than two minutes which the audience agreed wasn't really a talent. Another boy, Matthew, juggled five balls at once. The winning acts were the ventriloquism and juggling.

After the show, the student council committee provided pizza, tacos, fried chicken, hot dogs, cheeseburgers, and fries. They also had cupcakes, cookies, muffins, chocolate, and juice. Everyone ate and socialized after the show.

It was a memorable event for Kelly. She loved being the emcee and hoped to put on another show soon. She was exhausted when she got home. She ran straight to her bedroom as soon as she got back. She later changed into her pajamas and jumped into her bed. As she got settled in bed, she looked out the window at the stars.

Kelly believed that she could shine as bright as those stars by making a difference in a positive way. She eventually came up with a solution. She would be nice to Amelia even if Amelia wasn't very nice to her. This would set a good example.

The next day Kelly called her two best friends from Montana, Lola and Kristina. They had a long conversation about life, school, and the latest news.

There was a lot of cool stuff going on in her old neighborhood like fundraisers and contests. Kelly used to go to these events every year with her family, so she felt sad that she couldn't go this time. But she also felt determined to make new memories and have fun in her new home.

Chapter 5

THE SCIENCE PROJECT

Kelly's school had a huge science fair every year where two people from different grades had to work together. The teachers picked each partner. For some reason, Amelia and Kelly were paired up. Kelly wondered, out of all the students in the school, how could she have gotten paired up with Amelia.

Their theme was the solar system. Kelly loved science so this was 'a piece of cake' for her. It was her intention to get an 'A' on this project, no matter who her partner was.

In order to work together, the girls had to decide where they wanted to meet.

Amelia insisted on Kelly coming to her house. Kelly didn't really care where the location was as long as they got the work done. So she agreed to meet at Amelia's house the next day. Kelly thought that they would have met at a place more public like the library but went along with it.

That afternoon, Kelly went shopping with her mom at the arts and crafts store to buy the supplies for the project. They bought crayons, markers, construction paper, loose leaf paper, a display board, glue, pencils, styrofoam balls, stars, and paint.

When she went home she drew a model of what she thought the solar system should look like.

After school the next day, Kelly went to Amelia's house with all the supplies. Kelly was nervous about being in the house alone with Amelia. Kelly knocked on the door and waited for a little while. A few minutes later Amelia opened the door and let her in. Kelly didn't know what to say or do, so she walked in and just stood there. Amelia broke the silence and asked, "You have all the stuff?" to which she responded, "Yes." They discussed the proposed model in detail and decided to get to work.

They started out by reviewing the plan for the model. Then they wrote down some fun facts about the solar system. They painted the balls to look like the planets. In that moment they were working as friends — not enemies. However, as soon as they were finished, Amelia told Kelly to leave, and that was the end of that.

Earlier that afternoon Amelia had been in need of a snack, so she put some pizza rolls into the oven and carelessly forget about them. The kitchen was on the second floor, but she had been working with Kelly on the first floor. After Kelly left, Amelia stayed in the living room downstairs to watch television.

Amelia was kind of happy that she got paired with Kelly, even though she didn't really like her, because it actually given her a chance of winning the science fair. Amelia loved to win. She wanted to impress her family. She wanted to show people that she was smart and capable of doing something right. She felt that people always doubted her and that was why she was so mean to others. She had to think that she was better than they were in order to make herself feel good.

After a while, Amelia went upstairs to call one of her friends on the cheerleading squad. They talked for about an hour. While she was on the phone, the timer for the pizza rolls went off. But she couldn't hear it because she was talking and laughing so loudly. Not good!

Chapter 6

THE FIRE

Kelly was about a block away when she noticed that she had forgotten her notebook at Amelia's house.

So she turned around and ran back to the house. As she approached, she saw smoke coming out of the second floor window. She could hear someone screaming for help. Amelia burned the pizza rolls badly, so she threw water at the oven while it was still on. It was a terrible idea, but she did it in a moment of panic. Water caught one of the electrical cords. Then it sparked and started a fire.

Kelly wanted to help, but she did not know what to do. She knew that this situation was very risky, and she didn't want to make any mistakes or make it any worse.

Kelly looked around and she found a ladder outside of the garage. She pushed the heavy ladder with all her strength, and she set it near the window that Amelia was screaming through. She said, " Stay calm! Don't move !" The ladder wobbled, but Kelly kept holding on which was incredibly brave.

Neighbors gathered in panic saying, "Get down from there! You might get hurt!" some said. Kelly told Amelia to grab her hand. Amelia hesitated at first, but grabbed Kelly's hand as Kelly helped her down. They both reached the ground safely. The neighbors clapped as Kelly was named a hero. Amelia just stood still in disbelief.

The fire truck appeared and the firefighters asked if anyone else was in the house. They started spraying their hoses at the flames.

"Thank God we are safe," Amelia said while trying to take a deep breath. Thankfully, the fire department was able to preserve the entire first floor.

Amelia gave Kelly a big hug for helping her and apologized for the way that she had treated her. "Well, the truth is that I am very insecure," she said. "People always doubt me, so I pick on smaller people so that people won't focus on me. I am really sorry though, especially because you just saved my life. I guess I shouldn't judge other people before I get to know them."

Kelly forgave Amelia and said, "I hope we can be friends." "Of course," Amelia said.

A fireman came out and asked for Amelia's parents.

"They are on their way", replied Amelia,

"Your second floor is in really bad shape! You should be more careful when you use electrical appliances," the fireman said.

He told Kelly that what she did was very brave. He said, "this world needs more people like you. You were a real hero today." She was then invited to a town meeting later that night by the fire department.

Amelia's parents came rushing home worried sick.

Amelia said, "I'm fine! You should thank Kelly for rescuing me."

Amelia's dad said, "Thank you for saving my little girl."

Amelia's mom said, "Well, we have no place to stay while they repair the damages to the second floor. This is terrible. What are we going to do?"

"Excuse me Mr. and Mrs. Redison, my family has extra room in our house. I'm sure my parents wouldn't mind if you stayed awhile," said Kelly.

"Thank you darling. We appreciate your generosity. We will discuss it over with your parents first," said Mrs. Redison.

Kelly smiled and nodded.

"Really great, thank you so much!" said Amelia excitedly. "You know you are the friend I never wanted. I saw you on the first day and I thought that I could never be friends with you, but now that I know you, I am so glad that we are becoming friends."

When Kelly's parents heard about what happened, they were so proud and knew that this would be good for the girls.

At the town meeting that evening, Kelly was awarded a certificate from the mayor for her bravery.

Chapter 7

A TEMPORARY PLACE

After living under the same roof for just two days, Kelly and Amelia had to face going to school together and showing everyone that a so-called nerd could be friends with a cheerleader. Kelly's mom usually dropped her off at school. Two girls from two different worlds getting out of the same car. They walked into the school yard. Amelia's heart pounded as she thought of what the others would say. Kelly used her position as student council president to her advantage. She would ensure that anyone who was unkind be disciplined.

The school bell rang and Amelia's heart raced when she arrived in homeroom. Her classmates joked and laughed. In her mind everything was moving very slowly. But the kids were not laughing at her. She was so distracted that she got confused as her name was called for attendance. Not knowing what to say, she mumbled "Yes?"

After homeroom, the rest of the day passed by without incident. She noticed that nobody really cared about who she was friends with. It was all in her head. After school, Kelly and Amelia decided to go shopping with the rest of the cheerleaders. They had a great time. At nights after they both finished their homework, they played games or watched the latest episodes of their favorite show on television.

Amelia and Kelly gradually became best of friends because they hung out so much. Even though they were very different, they learned a lot about each other which made them closer.

Amelia had enjoyed her time at the Netti's house over the weeks, but it was quickly drawing to a close. Her house had been repaired and was as good as new. Kelly was really sad that Amelia had to leave because they were having so much fun together.

They had become like sisters. Although Amelia had to leave, their friendship wasn't over. They kept hanging out after school as best friends would.

Chapter 8

LIVE ON!

So all in all Amelia and Kelly became very good friends. They had a rocky start, but a scary experience brought them together. But it doesn't have to take a scary experience to be kind to each other. Not judging others based on appearances is the key to building friendships.

Kelly started to enjoy living in California. She made many memories with Amelia and her new friends. From then on, Amelia gained confidence and decided to have a new positive attitude towards life.

Later on, Kelly graduated from Harvard and became a successful pediatrician. She loves her job and teaches her patients to always be nice to others.

Amelia eventually became a gymnast and has won many medals.

Amelia and Kelly wrote this poem together and had it framed:

At times, life feels just like a race

Everyone gunning for first place

But if you stop to reevaluate

You will find that there's no room for hate.

About the Author

My name is Ashley-Rae Stewart. I was born in Jamaica, and I came to America at a young age. I grew up in New York. I live with my parents and my older sister.

I love reading, writing, and learning new things. I was always told that if you have a dream, don't just dream about it. Achieve it. It is awesome to have people in your life like family and friends who inspire you. Seeing kids getting bullied in school inspired me to write this book. My parents also told me it would be a good thing to always make a difference in the community, one way or another. In elementary and middle school, some kids I came in contact with were not so nice. I want to show people that you might need the person that you bully to help you out one day. So let's put an end to bullying! Spread love not hate!

CPSIA information can be obtained
at www.ICGtesting.com
Printed in the USA
FSOW04n2325101117
40979FS